Pri

E
MAY
JUS

Mayer, Mercer

Just me and my
babysitter.

D1573321

JUST ME AND MY BABYSITTER

BY MERCER MAYER

A GOLDEN BOOK • NEW YORK
Western Publishing Company, Inc., Racine, Wisconsin 53404

MCMXCIII

When Mom and Dad go out, the babysitter comes.

My little sister cries, but I do

Mom says I'm the babysitter's big helper.

I take the babysitter's coat
and hang it in the closet.

When it's time for supper
I show her where Mom keeps
the pots and pans.

I eat everything she gives me,
even if I don't like it.

I fill up the sink . . .

. . . and help her do the dishes.

Then we give my little sister a bath.
I keep her from crying.

I dry my little sister and help her put on her pajamas.

Then we put her to bed,
just me and my babysitter.

Now the work is over
and we can have some fun.
We make some popcorn.

We play checkers.
I am nice to my babysitter.
I let her win sometimes.

Then we watch a movie.
I let her choose.

She reads me a bedtime story.
I am very good.
I go right to sleep.

We have a good time,
just me and my babysitter.